I0610841

Ron Mueller

❧ Quiet Rabbit ☙

By: *Ron Mueller*

Around the World Publishing LLC
Cincinnati, Ohio

This story is a work of fiction. Names, characters, places, and incidents either are products of the author's imagination or are used fictitiously. Any resemblance to actual events or locales or persons, living or dead, is entirely coincidental.

Quiet Rabbit ©

All rights reserved, including the right of reproduction, in whole or in part in any form.

ISBN 13: 978-1-68223-414-0

Distributed by Ingram
Cover Design By: Ron Mueller
Cover Picture By: Hien Mueller

The Stories of Taelo are set in the distant past, long before the time currently given as to when people migrated into the western hemisphere.

This is purposely done since the stories are meant to engage the reader in a story and not relate exact history.

The adventures of Taelo and Golden Hawk provide the backdrop for stories featuring the values of treating others as you wish to be treated, of responsibility, integrity, honesty and of contribution, and the joy of learning.

&Dedicated to Marlene Hart the sister that I always wanted. &

<u>*Quiet Rabbit*</u>

Quiet Rabbit walked slowly behind and took in the orange, yellow and red of the leaves. The bright red leaves on one bush caught her eye and she wondered what name it had. She ran her hand through the tan waving grasses. She looked into a cloudless sky at a lone eagle gliding in a graceful seemingly effortless dance with the wind.

She pulled her favorite jacket snuggly around her as the gust reminded her that the season was chilling, and the cold season was ahead.

She had fallen behind as she absorbed what to her were the wonders of her world. She hurried forward to catch up with her parents.

They were holding hands and talking quietly to each other. Quiet Rabbit could not hear what they were saying but it did not matter. The way they were walking, the way they were talking, and the way they looked at each other was what Quiet Rabbit absorbed.

She knew that the bond, the force, the way they were one, was what she wanted for herself. To her it seemed that the two reinforced each other and together they were powerful, they were whole. She felt the warmth as if the two harbored the flames of a fire.

Quiet Rabbit ran ahead past them, until she reached a rocky open area along the lake bank. She looked around for some flat rocks that she could skip across the water. She giggled as her skipping stone was passed by one that went much farther than hers.

Her father had been given the name Flat Stone at his naming ceremony after he selected a flat stone from the edge of the naming blanket, but he was now known as Fast Skimmer for the speed of his running and his ability to skip his stones farther than anyone in the Elk Clan. He was also one of the best hunters in the Clan.

He was friends with Red Oak and Grey Fox Running. The three were the lead hunters for the clan.

He had told her mother and her that this was his departure walk with the two most beautiful women in his life.

He, Red Oak and Gray Fox Running were taking the hunters out on a long hunt. The Clan needed a fresh supply of meat to make it through the coming cycle. The hunters would be gone for at least one moon.

She felt the exhilaration flow through her as he picked her up and spun around with her in the air. They laughed together for the whole time.

The evening ended with them sitting together around White Swan's fire and sharing stories of long hunts in the past and of past exploits that they had shared.

The next day her father, Grey Fox Running and Red Oak led the hunting parties out for their annual long hunt. They would bring back enough meat to feed the Elk Horn Clan until the warm season.

She and her mother both wished all the hunters good hunting. The better the hunt went, the sooner the hunters came home.

Their return would be the trigger to prepare to travel to the seasonal gathering of all the Elk sub-clans.

The sun cycles seemed long and the moon cycles even longer. Finally, a runner came in with the news that the long hunters were returning.

She and her mother had marked a stick each evening as the sun left for the night and yielded to the sky lit by the twinkling of the many ancestors and the huge white lady of the night. They laughed together about the fact that they were Fast Skimmer's beautiful women, but he was their strong handsome man.

She and her mother spent many hours preparing goods that could be traded at the fall clan gathering.

A scout had returned and let the Clan know that the long hunters were returning. She and her mother and the rest of the Clan stood at the edge of the village waiting for their arrival.

A cheer went up when everyone saw at least six heavily loaded travois being pulled toward them.

Quiet Rabbit scanned the entire convoy but did not see the figure she was searching for. She looked up at her mother when the hand on her shoulder began to squeeze her to the point it hurt.

She had never seen her mother's face look so colorless. She took in the tears running down her face mother's face. Then her mother pushed her away and began to run toward the returning hunters.

Quiet Rabbit did not know what was wrong, but she ran after her mother. She had her father's running skill and easily caught up. She did not understand but a deep fear rose up and almost choked her.

Her mother ran toward Grey Fox Running.

Quiet Rabbit saw him turn and say something to Red Oak and then stepped aside to let the returning hunters proceed toward the camp.

She watched as her mother briefly looked at Red Oak and then continued to run towards Grey Fox Running.

There was one lone travois being pulled in the last position. The person pulling the travois stopped and put it down as her mother approached.

Grey Fox Running signaled for the hunter to go on.

Her mother knelt and slowly untied the elk skin wrapped around the figure. She reached out and touched the elk skin. She noted that the elk skin had been processed and felt soft and smooth.

The fur had been turned inward as was the custom. She knew that the spirit within was to be treated gently.

Her mother looked up at Grey Fox Running and thanked him for the respect that had been shown to Fast Skimmer.

Quiet Rabbit watched as her mother, true to her name cried silently as she leaned forward to put her hand on her father's face.

Tears were running down her own cheek as she stood frozen in her tracks. She welcomed the strong hands that lifted her.

She looked directly into Grey Fox Running's eyes and was surprised to see tears. He was a warrior, a hunter but he had lost one of his lifelong friends and he had to be the one to share this with his friend's mate and daughter.

She felt a surge of emptiness. A void filled her mind. She was glad that Grey Fox Running kept holding her.

Quiet Rabbit watched as White Swan and Floating Cloud arrived and comforted her mother. White Swan urged her mother to walk with her back to camp. Floating Cloud closed the elk skin cover and Grey Fox Running pulled the travois and followed the women.

******

The next moon cycle was one of the hardest Quiet Rabbit could remember. Her mother would not talk. She would walk most of the day and cry.

Quiet Rabbit went to her grandmother, Floating Cloud, seeking understanding and company.

Floating Cloud told her the story of how she too had lost her mate. At that time, she was pregnant with Silent Pool. Her husband, Proud Cougar, had gone fishing and had accidently been in the territory of a brown bear. He had only his fishing knife to defend himself, but he had killed the bear. In the ferocious fight he was mortally wounded.

He had staggered back to their camp carrying the fish he had gone to catch for dinner. He died in her arms, shortly after making it back.

****

Floating Cloud assured Quiet Rabbit that her mother would recover.

Immediately after the story, Quiet Rabbit went back to her mother and gave her a hug. She knew how hard it must be for her mother to have lost her soul mate.

Silent Pool was determined to overcome her grief. She had a daughter to care for but the grief, like the black of night, would come to the surface to pull her into the dark.

She would lose track of time. She would lose herself as she went about her daily chores. She worked exceptionally hard to prepare for the Elk clan gathering. She knew that she had to have enough goods so that she could take care of her daughter.

She knew she had to recover. The clan would soon leave for the seasonal clan meeting. For the sake of Quiet Rabbit, she had to make sure the family remained in good standing.

One morning, Silent Pool decided to get fresh water to make a rabbit stew for the morning meal. Stew always helped her to face the day. She asked her mother to go to the lake with her.

The sun was rising behind her and up ahead the clear pool of water awaited her. She looked up at the clear blue sky. It reminded her of her last walk with Fast Skimmer. A smile came to her lips, she turned to let her mother know about her memory, but she tripped on a windblown limb and staggered and fell backwards. She still had as smile on her lips as her head hit a fist sized stone.

Floating Cloud had been several paces behind Silent Pool and watched her trip and hit her head. She rushed forward and cradled her in her arms.

Silent Pool briefly opened her eyes, quietly muttered the words, "I am with him. Take good care of her." She then closed her eyes and let out a long breath. In a rapid instance, she was gone!

****

Floating Cloud sat with Silent Pool's head on her lap and quietly cried. She knew that Silent Pool had gone to where she wanted to be.

She would need to gently let Quiet Rabbit know. She promised herself that she would take care of Quiet Rabbit like she was her own daughter.

Quiet Rabbit woke as the sun touched her cheek and warmed it. She shielded her eyes to see if her mother was out by the cooking fire.

She got up and walked out hoping to get something to eat. No one was about.

She went to her grandmother's shelter, but it was empty.

White Swan walked up and told her to come to her camp breakfast.

Quiet Rabbit knew immediately that something bad had happened.

Taelo was sitting by the fire ring and patted the seat next to him.

A few moments later her grandmother, appeared as she came back from having left Silent Pool with the clan's seer. He would prepare her for her trip to the ancients.

Quiet Rabbit took one look and knew that her grandmother had news she did not want to hear.

The loss of her father had saddened Quiet Rabbit. He had been her play partner. The loss of her mother broke her heart. Her mother had been her comforter and confident.

Quiet Rabbit felt so alone.

Floating Cloud shared Silent Pool's last words and hugged Quiet Rabbit.

****

Two sun cycles later the clan left for the annual Elk Clan gathering.

Quiet Rabbit knew that the Elk clan now boasted seven prospering sub-clans.

Her father had told her that the success of the Clan was due in large part to solid leaders, to their hunters and to a group of elders, who brought balance to the hotter heads. It was also due to their willingness to share their resources to balance out the vital food stores prior to each winter. Ensuring each clan had enough food for the winter was one of the most critical tasks during the meeting.

She knew that for the last several seasons the Elk Horn Clan had out produced all the other clans by a significant amount. They had generously shared food supplies with the other sub-clans.

This year the Elk Horn clan was loaded with an over-abundance of dried fish, elk, rabbit, moose, and other food stuffs. Their supply of leather goods, baskets, general utensils, woven cloth, various tools, fishhooks, stone ax heads and clothing made them the most prosperous members of the clan. This abundance had so loaded them down that they were the last to arrive at the meeting valley.

Her mother had prepared well. She had told Quiet Rabbit that the two of them would need to be hard traders. They now had to make their own way.

****

Quiet Rabbit took in the scene below them.

The early morning was still. All was quiet. The light wispy campfire smoke from each family camp rose straight into the still morning air like white worms dancing slowly in the wind. The undulation of the parallel plumes of smoke seemed to be orchestrated as they danced in unison. The sun, rising over the far horizon caused them to change colors of pinks and yellows and it seemed as if the plumes were alive.

The Wise Owl their leader stopped at the top of the hill to look out across the valley.

It was a scene that caused everyone in the Elk Horn Clan to stop and take in the beauty.

Quiet Rabbit immediately took in the grouping of campfires. It indicated all the other sub clans, but theirs, had already arrived and set up camp. The Elk Horn Clan would have to take the place farthest away from the river and up along the hillside.

Wise Owl stood overlooking the valley below. She heard him comment that he really disliked having arrived so late.

Because of their abundant wealth, it had taken them longer to pack up and they had traveled slower than anticipated because of their load. Now he stood contemplating what he should have his sub clan do.

Quiet Rabbit stood with her grandmother taking in the sight of the Elk Clan gathering.

She listened as Taelo suggested they camp on the other side of the lake. None of the Elk sub clans had ever camped there because of the small stream feeding the lake.

He pointed out the advantages and was given the task of build a bridge across the stream and then signaling success.

Wise Owl decided to give it a try. He liked the idea of walking by all the camp sites showing off his Clan's richness and then proceeding to an excellent campsite on the edge of the lake.

He gave Taelo the task to build a bridge across the stream and then signal success via a fire with green leaves thrown in to send up a white plume.

Later she watched as the signal, set by Taelo and his team of bridge builders, rose into the air and signaled that the other side was ready for the Elk Horn Clan.

She along with the rest of the Elk Hide Clan let out a loud hurrah. It made her feel so good. She would long remember having her spirit uplifted.

She and her Grandmother walked proudly through the Elk camp and across to the other side of the lake.

Both had a great supply of goods to trade and looked forward to the gathering and the bartering that would take place.

A few sun cycles later, Floating Cloud asked her if she were willing to leave the Elk Horn Clan and move into the Elk clan. She went on to explain that Grey Fox Running was to be the new leader of the Elk Clan and that she thought it would be good for the two of them to change clans and join the Elk Clan.

Though very surprised, Quiet Rabbit immediately agreed. One of her best friends was Grey Fox Running's son. She wanted to be where he was, and she did not want to go back to the place that would constantly remind her of her father's and mother's death.

The change of clan to the original parent Elk Clan was a welcome one for her. It took her away from the sorrow she associated with the Elk Hide Clan.

The fact that she and all Elk Clan members were immediately on food rations was a surprise that alarmed her.

Most of the food that she and her grandmother had accumulated through hard trading was distributed to each of the Elk Clan families by Grey Fox Running and Red Oak.

Every person in the Clan had about the same amount of food. Quiet Rabbit knew that the amount would not be enough to take them through the coming cold cycle.

The journey to their new home was to be long and challenging.

She watched as Taelo and Golden Hawk became the inspiration for the young members of the Elk Clan.

She did not go out to hunt and scout as they did, but she organized those who stayed with the moving caravan, to gather berries and to fish the streams and small lakes they were passing.

She in her own right gained the respect of the Elk Clan members. White Swan was like an aunt to her and encouraged her efforts.

She found the journey to the coast long and tedious.

Taelo and Golden Hawk broke the tediousness when they found the honey tree. The entire Elk Clan gathered around the very large twisted and exceptionally knurled oak tree. The amount of honey exceeded anything that had been experienced before.

High overhead an eagle let out a loud cry.

Quite Rabbit soon came to know each time a special event was happening to Taelo. An eagle would fly overhead and let out a long cry.

She was there listening when White Swan, Taelo's mother insisted the clan stop and wait for Taelo to return from an excursion he and Golden Hawk had taken. White Swan explained that the cry of the eagle meant that Taelo was experiencing a special event.

Late that night, as the Elk Clan waited, Taelo and Golden Hawk entered camp pulling a travois loaded with a large elk and the hides of two exceptionally large dire wolves.

The elk provided the margin of food that relieved the leaders concern about feeding the clan for the near term.

She helped White Swan and her grandmother as they fed Taelo and Golden Hawk.

She was amazed as she listened to their account of fighting three very large dire wolves. She heard some of the old-seasoned hunters of the clan say that what the two had done was almost impossible.

****

Two sun cycles later, four hunters from Red Oak's hunting group brought the meat from a buffalo, two boar, four elk and the meat of numerous small game. She and the entire Elk Clan greeted them. It was now clear they would have enough food to continue their journey.

She hid with Taelo and Golden Hawk under a hide so they could stay up and listen to the stories about hunting with Red Oak. She had tears in her eyes because her father had hunted with Red Oak and had told many similar tales, as the one she now listened to.

****

The journey to the coast took longer than Quiet Rabbit had expected. When they finally arrived, Silent Hawk the acting clan leader, while Grey Fox Running was out on the long hunt asked White Swan to go down the coast to look for a good winter camp. Everyone else would stay camped in their current location.

He would go up the coast and do the same.

Whoever found a good location would come back and lead the Elk Clan to their winter home.

Quiet Rabbit watched as White Swan, her sister Quiet Pheasant, Taelo and Golden Hawk jogged away down the beach.

She knew that it was a special situation for a woman to be given such respect and authority.

White Swan returned a few sun cycles later and let the clan know that she had found an excellent home location.

There was confusion when a group said they should wait for Silent Hawk to return before deciding what to do.

White Swan told them to follow her, turned and walked back down the beach.

Quiet Rabbit grabbed her grandmother. They were among the first to follow White Swan to Elk Clan's new home location.

White Swan guided the planning, locating, and building of the main lodge and arranging the layout of the camp.

This was a period that Quiet Rabbit worked harder than she had ever done before. It was a period where everyone was needed to contribute to getting ready to survive the winter.

****

The main lodge was just completed when Red Oak returned with his long hunt team. He told of his encounter with a group of raiding hunters from the people called the Others.

This alarmed the Elk Clan Members.

Quite Rabbit observed that White Swan did not seem to have the same reaction.

A short time later a very battered group of long hunters led by Brave Dear returned. They had no additional food. Instead, they told the story of being hunted by a large pack of dire wolves.

Quiet Rabbit looked over at Taelo and Golden Hawk and again wondered how the two had bested the dire wolves. The two had gone up the very valley that Brave Dear and his group had traveled and had probably met part of the same pack of dire wolves.

****

Though opposed by many of the Elk clan elders, White Swan convinced them that she should go and meet with the clan of Others.

White Swan, Quiet Pheasant, Taelo and Golden Hawk took a travois loaded with food and gifts and went north along the coast.

Quiet Rabbit shouted encouragement as the four left the camp. She held a deep belief that Taelo's and Golden Hawk's presence would be the deciding factor.

Quiet Rabbit and her grandmother kept a daily watch out to the north along the beach. She was at first alarmed as she watched White Swan and Quiet Pheasant returning alone along the beach.

She rushed out to greet them and was greatly relieved when she was told that Taelo and Golden Hawk had been received like heroes. Later she laughed heartedly when White Swan shared the story of Taelo defending her against a rude and rough bear of a man.

****

The approaching winter solstice brought so many memories of long ago. Quiet Rabbit had kept herself busy and engaged in preparing the winter camp. Now she found herself at an emotional low point. She talked quietly to Floating Cloud about her grief.

Then, she heard the scream of the eagle, not from the sky but out along the beach.

She dropped everything and ran out to the edge of the camp.

The scene was confusing.

Red Oak and Grey Fox Running and the long hunters were gathered in one group.

The Elk Clan members were standing behind White Swan.

And out by a large log were two smaller figures in front of four very powerful looking men of the Others.

Quiet Rabbit watched as the groups converged and greeted each other. She knew that something very unusual was occurring.

The winter solstice went from a low feeling to a high one.

Her best friend was back.

Her mood changed and she enjoyed the winter solstice much more than she had thought possible.

A moon cycle after the Solstice she learned that Taelo and Golden Hawk had secretly left the camp. Their new friend and protector, Burly Bear of the Others had followed them in hopes of helping them.

Quiet Rabbit listened to Floating Cloud, White Swan and Quiet Pheasant talking around the cooking fire as they discussed the actions of Taelo and Golden Hawk.

She agreed with them when they highlighted that Burly Bear going out to find his two friends made all of them feel better.

It was hard for her not to worry about the two. The moon cycles passed slowly. More than two moon cycles had passed since Taelo left the camp. The members of the Elk Clan were once again facing a food shortage.

Quiet Rabbit discussed the situation with Floating Cloud. She wondered what she could do to help. She started going out with her sling and she would periodically bring back a rabbit or squirrel.

It was not much but it provided the occasional good meal. She gained confidence in her ability to provide food for herself and her grandmother as her skill with the sling slowly improved.

She was near to Grey Fox Running's camp when a scout came in and said there were people coming in along the coast from the south.

She and her grandmother were standing next to Grey Fox Running at the top of the spit cliffs, when he laughed and said that it could only be Burly Bear, Golden Hawk and Taelo.

She was among the group that went out to greet the returning three. She realized that the meat that was on their sled would tide the whole clan through the coming spring.

Spring was a welcome relief from one of the coldest winters the clan had experienced. Spring was always a frustrating season in that food remained scarce. But Taelo let everyone know that a herd of buffalo spent the cold season in the valley on the other side of the mountains.

****

Quiet Rabbit was among the first supporters when Taelo and Golden Hawk began building a seaside version of their famous fish trap. She organized all the younger members of the camp.

She, her new friends Busy Bee and Talking Wren, became the task masters of getting the necessary long poles and weaving the wooden barrier walls ready to be installed.

The success of the fish trap was an unexpected reward for the Elk Clan. Food became abundant.

The capture of a very large shark in the fish trap made Taelo, Golden Hawk and Burley Bear very affluent young men. The hide was very valuable and each of the very large shark teeth were more valuable than a person's weight in salt.

She, Busy Bee, and Talking Wren were each given three shark teeth. Each got a large one, a medium size and a smaller one. They all knew that they had been singled out and recognized for having given the effort their support.

Quiet Rabbit looked at the three shark teeth given to her by Taelo. She took them and showed them proudly to Floating Cloud who agreed with Taelo that Quiet Rabbit had earned them.

****

The summer season proved to be as generous as Taelo.

The cliff that projected out into the ocean and was the home to thousands of birds yielded not only an abundance of eggs but blueberries as well.

The flat stone area along the cliff base became a place to evaporate the salt water and make salt.

The Elk Clan produced more sea salt than she had ever seen in one place. She, Busy Bee, and Talking Wren had their own salt making area that they managed. They became wealthy salt owners.

Quiet Rabbit led both the egg hunting and blueberry picking. She helped Floating Cloud make a jam of the blue berries by slowly cooking out most of the water and adding a small amount of honey.

****

She was surprised when she, Busy Bee and Talking Wren were approached by White Swan and Quiet Pheasant and told that they should consider going on the long hunt with Taelo and Golden Hawk.

The thought of going on a long hunt thrilled her and her friends.

To go on a long hunt with Taelo was beyond what she could have dreamt of.

A few sun cycles later the long hunt teams were organized. The elders had agreed to one additional long hunt team. It would have three women on that team.

They named Little Otter as the leader of that team.

Quite Rabbit was surprised at the choice of leader. Taelo and Golden Hawk both were better leaders than Little Otter. She looked at both and knew that though the team was being discounted the two were quiet but looking confident.

The long hunt teams left camp.

Taelo commented that their team had been given the worst location.

Burley Bear spoke up and said that he would need to go by the camp of the Others to pick up some of his hunting gear.

Though nothing was said, Quiet Rabbit immediately knew that Burley Bear, Taelo and Golden Hawk were guiding the team in a new direction. She was not sure what they were doing but she knew Burley Bear already had all the hunting gear he needed.

Quiet Rabbit was surprised to have the entire clan of Others out waiting for their hunt team. She watched as Taelo walked up to a badly damaged old man and gave him hug.

Taelo introduced the long hunt team to Broken Spear, the seer of the Others. He also introduced Silver Arrow as the leader of the Others.

Quiet Rabbit walked up and gave Broken Spear a hug just like Taelo had given. She put her hand on the shoulder of Silver Arrow and added her name. She was surprised that he smelled faintly of pine and lavender.

Busy Bee and Talking Wren followed her lead.

She was amazed by the large cave found by Taelo for the Clan of Others. It was more of an open area that looked out at an expansive valley from under the mountain, than a cave.

A waterfall poured cold water into a hot spring basin. The result was a warm water pool. This was a luxury she wished was available to the Elk clan.

Taelo led the team out to it and proceeded to get in and enjoy the hot water.

Quiet Rabbit was the first to join in.

The team was not only welcomed but enjoyed a celebration evening dinner and a long story-telling session. Taelo and Golden Hawk told stories about each other and about Burley Bear.

It was clear by the hooting and stomping that the Clan enjoyed the stories that made fun of Burley Bear.

The tight bond that existed among her and the rest of the Elk hunters grew to a new depth for Quiet Rabbit.

She was where she wanted to be.

Broken Spear and Silver Arrow, the leader of the others informed the team that Meadow Flower, the future mate of Burley Bear was joining the team.

This, they added, assured that each person and their mate would be on the same long hunt team.

Quiet Rabbit was surprised by the statement but took this as a sign that she would need to act to assure she got the right mate.

She knew she was on the right team, now she was going to make sure she ended up with the right mate.

The team left the cave of the others to hunt in part of the clan's hunting ground.

Broken Spear had warned Taelo that the team faced an unknown challenge and that they would help one of the Other's hunt teams. Both action he said would distinguish this team as a special team.

A few suns later, Taelo advised that they had reached the lake suggested by Broken Spear to be the site of their hunt.

Little Otter suggested that they hunt in two teams. He designated Taelo and Golden Hawk to lead the hunt teams. He assigned Burley Bear to be on Taelo's team and he would be on Golden Hawk's team.

He pointed to a tree about fifty spear lengths away and said that the women would be assigned to the two teams based on the order that they finished the race.

The race was ready to begin, Quiet Rabbit knew she was among the fastest of the women but knew that Talking Wren often beat her. When the race started, she was surprised that Busy Bee was running as fast as she was.

She was determined to win.

She was determined to hunt with Taelo.

She put that vision in her head, her feet flew, and she pulled ahead. She was several spear lengths in front of Busy Bee as she crossed the finish line.

She knew that she would hunt with Taelo and that eventually she would fulfill Broken Spear's prediction of being Taelo's mate. It was she decided the will of the Ancestors and of her mother and father.

She did not know it at the time, but each one of the women ended up hunting with their eventual mates.

She took note that Busy Bee had made it in second and was on Golden Hawk's hunt team. She knew he was Busy Bee's target mate.

She also knew that Talking Wren had seemed to run slower than normal. She was a good friend.

****

The long hunt teams all had good success, but Little Otter's long hunt team doubled the combined meat production of all the other long hunt teams put together.

Quiet Rabbit learned from Little Otter on his return from delivering the first load of meat to the Clan that all long hunt teams were doing well, but he proudly boasted that their team doubled the combined meat production of all the other long hunt teams.

He also shared that he had been praised for his great leadership. But that he had made the point that the women on the team were the key factor in their hunting success.

Quiet Rabbit cut off a piece of the buffalo hump that was roasting on the spit and presented it to Little Otter with a thank you.

Talking Wren was at his side and her influence over his behavior was clear to Quiet Rabbit and Busy Bee.

Quiet Rabbit and Busy Bee later shared with White Swan, Quiet Pheasant and Floating Cloud that they had each hunted with the teams and had learned to place the spear into the chest of the buffalo from their hunt partners.

White Swan congratulated them and then shared that she had taught this hunting technique to Grey Fox Running and Fast Skimmer. Red Oak though an excellent hunter was not fast enough to use this hunting technique. This hunting technique was passed to her by her father.

She was sure that Fast Skimmer would have loved to have taught Quiet Rabbit, but White Swan said she was happy that Taelo had done so.

With tears of happiness, Quiet Rabbit went out to her boulder by the edge of the water.

She was sure she and Taelo would walk, they would talk, they would hold hands the way her parents had done. She knew she and Taelo would have what her parents shared with one another.

She smiled and looked out into the harbor and thanked both for having been the parents they had been.

The End

Thank you for reading to this point!

About the Author

Ronald E. Mueller
remwriter95@gmail.com
Ron grew up in what is now Flint River
State Park in Southeast Iowa. The 170-
year-old house Ron lived in is built into a
hillside. It faces a 125-foot-high cliff
towering over the little Flint River. The
house and the land talked to him about; the
passing of time, the struggle to conquer the
land, the struggles people faced and the wonder of nature.

He climbed the cliffs, crawled into the caves, dove from the
swimming rock, collected clams from the bottom of the pond,
gigged and skinned frogs for their legs. He trapped muskrats for
fur, hunted raccoon in the dead of night, and with only a stick
hunted rabbits in the dead of winter.

His young life was outdoors, and nature tested him.

He walked to a one room stone schoolhouse uphill both ways.
A stern but warm-hearted teacher, Mrs. Henry was instrumental
in shaping his character as she shepherded him from the fourth to
the eighth grade.

It was a great way to grow up.

Ron graduated from Burlington, High School, went to
Vietnam in the Navy. He graduated from The University of
South Florida with a master's degree in engineering, worked for
thirty eight years for Procter and Gamble, traveled around the
world thirty times.

He has remained happily married for more than fifty years.
His daughter and his two sons are all successful and his three
grandchildren have all graduated.

His wife has humored and supported him as he became a full
time professional story teller.

His experiences inter-twined with snippets of fantasy lend
themselves to the adventures he leads the reader through.

Books by Ron Mueller

Fiction Series
The Taelo Series
The Early Years
The Golden Feather
Journey of Discovery
Dangerous Passage
Condor Clan Slingers
Circumvention
The Journey of Sages
Future Leaders Journey
Taelo Collection

A Taelo Story
White Swan and Quiet Pheasant
The Child's Name
Floating Cloud
Quiet Rabbit
Busy Bee
Little Otter & Talking Wren
Broken Spear
Burley Bear & Meadow Flower
Taelo Story Collection

The Alex Evercrest Series
The River Front
The Girl on The Grill
Missing
Maggot
Racist
Votive Candles
Windy City
Country Road
Pool of Blood
Sins of the Daughter
Body Parts
The Skull Collector
The Vanishing
The Shadow Fighter
Moonshine
Grief's Trajectory
The Magic Touch
Northern Lights
Alex Evercrest Heroine
Alex Evercrest Collection Two
New Direction
A Family Affair
Disruption
The St. Lebuinnus Church Murder

A Brian O'Neil Novel
Hawaiian Phoenix
Moon Curser
Death Broker

The Problem Solver Series
Solutions
Drug Lords

Border Crosser
The Problem Solver Collection

Science Fiction

The Savitar Series:
Journey's End
Savitar
Confluence
Savitar Series Collection

Bram Nielson Series
The Fold
The Message
Fold Wormhole
Negative Fold
Ripples in Time
Bram Nielson Collection

Single Science Fiction Books:
Current Past and Future
The Event
The Door
Viajante 7

https://www.remwriter95.net/

Published by: Around the World Publishing LLC.

www.ingramcontent.com/pod-product-compliance
Lightning Source LLC
Chambersburg PA
CBHW060602100726
47907CB00005B/1482